The Lost Umbrella
of Kim Chu

The Lost Umbrella of Kim Chu

by ELEANOR ESTES

illustrated by Jacqueline Ayer

A MARGARET K. MC ELDERRY BOOK

Atheneum   1978   New York

To Marjorie

Contents

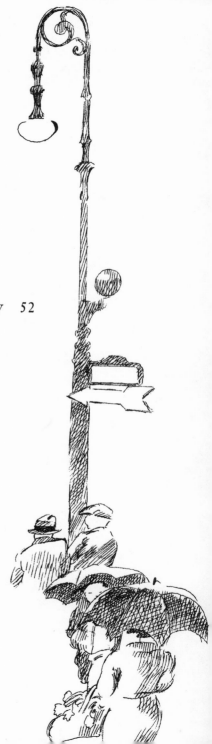

The Lost Umbrella
of Kim Chu

1

The Umbrella

ON FRIDAY, WHEN KIM CHU GOT OUT OF REGULAR SCHOOL OVER ON Bayard Street, it was raining only a little, scarcely more than a drizzle. Kim liked the feeling of the soft rain on her cheeks as she hurried off to Chinese School on Mott Street. Kim and many of her friends went to that little school every afternoon after regular school from Monday through Friday. There they learned the Chinese language, to read it and to write it . . . how to form the beautiful letters, what brushes and pens to use, what kind of ink and paper. Also they studied the long history of China. Chinese School lasted for one hour.

In Chinese School Kim's best friend was a girl named Mae Lee. She didn't go to the Bayard Street school, because she lived way away, on Staten Island, not in Chinatown where Kim lived. Mae Lee was there today, but she did not leave at a quarter past four when Kim did. She had some work to make up.

Down on the street, the rain was no longer a drizzle. It was pouring. And there was a strong wind that blew people's umbrellas inside out and whiplashed ladies' skirts around them. Kim saw that if you held an umbrella toward the wind it might not blow inside out. But she didn't have an umbrella anyway and in a minute her straight black hair was plastered to her head as though it had been painted on her, and her bright red coat—all of her—was soaking, sopping wet.

Kim didn't live far from Chinese School. Her house was just around the corner on Park Row. It looked like all the other houses on the block, all built side by side, with no space in between. In spite of the driving rain, the outside door of her tenement was wide open as it always was except in blizzards and bitterly cold weather. But not much rain came in because of the elevated train tracks above on Park Row which, like a vast umbrella, sheltered the houses below.

Kim Chu lived on the second floor of her narrow house. There were two apartments on every floor and Kim's was in the back half. From the foot of the steep staircase you could see all the way up to a narrow hallway where there was a door into Kim's front room. This door was open, too, as it always was until all the family was home. Kim tore up the stairs.

"Look at me, how wet I am!" she cried merrily. "Grandmother, look!"

Kim Chu's grandmother was sitting in a straight chair, the only piece of furniture in this square room. The only other thing in the room was Kim's father's big, black umbrella that stood in a corner.

In this middle-of-the-house room there weren't any windows. But, through a door at the back, there was another room you could see into and that room had a window opening onto a fire escape.

Kim put her schoolbooks on the floor in the corner beside the big umbrella. "See, Grandmother?" she said. "They are not wet, only a little damp, because I kept them close to me, under my coat."

She spoke in Chinese and her grandmother answered in Chinese for that was the only language she spoke and understood. Kim shook out her wet hair and spattered the tan walls a little and even her grandmother's face.

Grandmother looked astonished tasting rain on her lips. It had been a long time since she had tasted rain. That was in China. She rarely went out here, only during the Chinese New Year's celebrations. Everybody went out then. Every year Kim's father danced inside the head of the New Year's dragon as it wound through the streets. But this past New Year's celebration, which had ushered in the Year of the Dragon, had been the best so far for Kim and her family. There had been a competition for the best design for the great long dragon, and Kim's father had won!

Because of this, he had been the guest of honor at a big banquet, and a gift had been bestowed upon him by the man who was called "the mayor of Chinatown." The gift was the huge black umbrella with a bamboo handle that was standing now in the corner of the square room.

This umbrella was the only one that the family owned. Because it had not been raining this morning when Kim's mother and father had left for the restaurant way uptown on 125th Street where they worked, they had not taken the umbrella. There it stood, nice and dry.

Kim said to her grandmother, "Now, I have to go to the library and return my books; they are due today. I won't be long."

She got her two library books from the room in back and went to the door. She could hear the rain come beating down. She could see the damp spot at the foot of the stairs and the wet trail she had left coming up them a few minutes ago. She paused and looked back at the big umbrella.

To look at this big, black umbrella one would not think it any different from any other man's big umbrella, many of which have bamboo handles. But it was the bamboo handle of the umbrella of Kim Chu's father that made his an especially important one. It had a secret to it.

The handle of this umbrella could be unscrewed, if you knew about it and knew the special twists and turns to make in order to unscrew it. If you did know how to do all of this, you would find, in the hollow of the bamboo handle, a miniature scroll. If you unwound the scroll, which was tied with a fragile, bright silken thread, you would find, in Chinese, these words—hand-lettered with a very fine brush in black ink and on paper of great delicacy:

This umbrella is presented by the people of Chinatown to Mr. Lin Chu, honoring him for his fierce and funny design for this year's dragon ushering in THE YEAR OF THE DRAGON.

At the bottom of the scroll there was a black and gold drawing of his fierce dragon.

Kim and her whole family, including her little sister Shoo-Shoo and Grandmother, had gone to the dinner party honoring her father. When the mayor of Chinatown presented her father with the special umbrella he said that another miniature scroll would be placed inside the bamboo handle each year that Kim's father designed the best and most beautiful dragon.

"May there be a hundred scrolls in there!" the mayor had said in exuberance.

Everybody had clapped and laughed at the idea of even the young Mr. Lin Chu living to the age of one hundred and thirty-five! That's the age one hundred miniature scrolls would make him. Even Grandmother had laughed but had not looked surprised.

Unless a person had been at that big dinner party for Kim's father, he would not have guessed the secret of the bamboo handle. It fitted together as tightly as the best of the Chinese puzzle boxes.

The remembrance of this celebration rushed through Kim's mind as she looked at the umbrella. She walked back into the room. "What is the use of an umbrella if it stands in a corner when it is raining outside?" she asked herself.

"Grandmother," she said. "It's still raining so hard out! I think I'll take the big umbrella. Then I will not get any wetter and the library books will stay dry."

Kim got the umbrella from the corner . . . it was almost as tall as she. But Grandmother did not like this idea of Kim Chu's. She was cross and the frown on her forehead deepened. "You will lose the umbrella," she said in Chinese.

"Oh, no! Grandmother," said Kim politely. "I never lose anything. I won't lose my father's big umbrella. Look at it! Such a huge one! How could I lose it? You will see. I will be back soon. *We* will be back soon . . . the bumbershoot and I."

Kim said the word "bumbershoot" in English and left her grandmother sitting on the straight chair, still looking cross but murmuring, "Bam Boo Shoot," over and over in puzzlement.

Kim walked down the steep stairway holding the umbrella upright in front of her like a sword so that she would not trip or make anybody else trip.

And she stepped outside in the rain with her father's fine, big umbrella.

2

Kim Chu and the Big Umbrella

DOWN ON THE STREET KIM OPENED UP THE UMBRELLA. SHE STOOD A moment outside of her house and looked up and down the street. Broken umbrellas like enormous wounded blackbirds lay in the gutters. But now the wind had died down so Kim did not have to struggle to keep her father's umbrella from blowing inside out. The rain was just as dense a rain as ever, though, and sheltered completely, Kim walked along happily in it. It poured off her umbrella in transparent sheets. Kim laughed. "I feel as though I am behind a waterfall," she thought.

She skirted around the biggest puddles on the sidewalk, not to keep her shoes dry—they were already sopping wet—but so that she would not fall into the upside-down world of a rain puddle and never get out of the sky there. Sometimes she raised the umbrella way way up so she could see out. But most of the time she walked hunched under it and avoided the puddles. People might think this was a walking umbrella that had two legs, Kim Chu's skinny little legs in black, ribbed stockings.

The library was not far away . . . just a half-block to the corner and then, around it, a very short block to go on East Broadway. On the way, just before reaching the corner, there was a moving picture house. Kim stopped for a minute to look at the awful pictures on the billboards outside. The names of the pictures were in English, so the words spoken in the pictures must be in English, too. The posters looked scary. Even if Kim had had the money she would not have gone in there.

So far the only moving pictures that Kim had seen were Chinese ones given in a little movie house on Mott Street. Sometimes she had

to close her eyes, not to look, for even these were scary. Her friend, Mae Lee, never closed her eyes. Probably she would not close her eyes for the fearful English movies either. She was a brave girl.

Kim Chu and Mae Lee had learned a lot from the Chinese moving pictures. They knew how to speak out of the corner of their mouths without moving their lips, knew how to show what they had in mind by the lift of an eyebrow, the flick of an eyelid, or a look of the eyes. They put all of this into practice in plays they acted in at Chinese School. Sometimes they made up their own plays, and that was fun, too. They were both going to be actresses when they grew up, they had decided.

Kim walked on. She wished that Mae lived in Chinatown and was walking along with her right now under this big umbrella. At the corner she stopped. She tilted her umbrella back and looked up at the elevated station—CHATHAM SQUARE. Two lines, the Second Avenue Line and the Third Avenue Line, came in here, one on the lower platform and the other way up on the top level, so this station was always busy.

People streamed onto the El trains and people streamed off them. It was always, "Hurry-up, hurry-up!" Then the trains would speed along the tracks and send sparks down below, especially in cold weather. Supposing her father's New Year's dragon went streaking down these tracks! What a sight that would be, shooting off fireworks into the smoky sky!

Maybe some day her mother and father would take her with them on the elevated train to where they worked. She had never been on an El. Once she and her whole family, except Grandmother, went

13

on a trolley ride across Brooklyn Bridge and back again. That was a ride! What sights they had seen! Ferryboats . . . all kinds of boats. But now, hurry, hurry, hurry to the library!

It was way after four o'clock, but not dark yet. Daylight saving time would be going on for one more week. Even so, the janitor had already turned on the two lights at the entrance to the library. Children were going in and coming out . . . some grown-ups, too. One grown-up, a man in a dark suit, a judge, perhaps, from City Hall which was not far away, pushed past Kim to get into the library and out of the rain. No wonder! He was soaking wet, as wet as Kim, and his trouser legs clung to him, for he did not have an umbrella.

He probably wanted one of those books on business that were on the first floor of the library for grown-ups to look things up in, how to get to be a mayor or a millionaire. Kim had seen those books marked BUSINESS. They were right beyond the books in Chinese. Once Kim had brought home some of these grown-up books in Chinese to Grandmother when the library teacher said she might like them. But Grandmother did not like them. She said they were not written in the Chinese language that she knew. She liked better for Kim to read her own library stories out loud to her, putting the English words into the Chinese that they both knew. She laughed a long time over the stories in a book named *Shen of the Sea*. So did Kim.

If that book were in, Kim would borrow it again and read it to Grandmother while they were waiting for Kim's mother and father and little Shoo-Shoo, whom they would pick up at Aunt Min's, where she stayed every day, on Mott Street. Then Grandmother would not be cross with her any more for having taken her father's big, black

14

umbrella out in the rain. And she would laugh instead and pat Kim's cheek with her trembling hand.

Kim closed the umbrella, shook it, and folded it neatly. She went up the long wide flight of stairs to the Children's Room. This room was her favorite place in all the world, with books standing on top of the shelves opened to bright pictures; and flowers . . . there were always pretty fresh flowers in vases on the desk and on the tops of the shelves. And there was a fishbowl, too, with a tadpole in it, along with the fishes, and the tadpole was growing a tail. It was taking him a long time. Happily she thought of seeing Mrs. Parks, the librarian, whom Kim and all the children called "library teacher," and of saying hello to her.

At the top of the stairs there was an umbrella rack, rectangular

in shape, with a little square for each umbrella. Kim put her father's tall umbrella in the back square on the left-hand side where it could not hide the little ones in front. How splendid the umbrella looked there, the king of the umbrellas! And, like a king who must have many secret hiding places for precious things, King Umbrella had one, too, in his handle!

There was a long line of children at the desk and Kim took her place in it, waiting for her turn. At first she was standing beside a little glassed-in office where, at one desk, torn books were mended and labels pasted into new ones. She could even smell the library paste. Once she had mended books in there. She had owed eight cents for keeping her books too long. Sometimes the library teacher let children who owed the library money work off their fine by mending books in that little room. The paste was in a round jar that had a round glass tube built into the middle of it where a little water kept the brush moist. Kim loved that room and the smell of that paste.

Perhaps she should be a library teacher when she grew up and not a mysterious actress who could speak with her eyes only or else side-mouth her words without moving her lips. She would talk this over with her friend, Mae Lee.

A big boy she didn't know was in the mending room now, sticking a clean pocket in the back of an old book. A friend of his was standing on the other side of the glass partition making faces at him, rolling his eyes, pulling his mouth down at the corners and into many weird shapes, also his nose, making the mender laugh so that he pasted the pocket in crooked. Kim wished that she was the one who owed the money and could be in there pasting in pockets and erasing marks.

But her books were not overdue. It was her turn now, her books were taken in, her card stamped "returned," and she went into the Children's Room. Three little boys, all dressed in shiny black raincoats with shiny black hats like firemen's helmets pushed past Kim to get out. They were laughing and they were saying, "Trip-trap-trip-trap . . . who's 'at walking over my bridge?" They were very little boys and they tore past the umbrella rack and down the stairs . . . trip-trap. In coats like theirs they didn't need any umbrella, big or little.

"Hello, Kim," the library teacher said. She knew just about everybody's name and everybody knew hers, "Mrs. Parks." She must have read every book in the library. If you couldn't find a good one, she always knew of one. But Kim found *Shen of the Sea* herself and then she also chose a book named *Emil and the Detectives* that Mrs. Parks said was very funny.

Kim got in line on the other side of the desk and had her books stamped to take home. On this side of the desk she could not smell the paste but she could see the little mending room. The boy was still pasting there. But the face-maker boy on the other side had gone. He must have gotten tired of waiting for his friend, thought Kim.

Kim hated to leave this warm and pretty, brightly lighted room. But anyway, she did have two good books. At the top of the stairs she thumbed through the book of *Emil and the Detectives* trying to find a funny place; and then, slowly, she went down the stairs. She forgot all about the big umbrella.

Outdoors, she still did not remember the umbrella because it had stopped raining while she was in the library. The rain puddles should have reminded her. But they didn't. She was still thinking about her books, the smell of paste and the lovely flowers. She just didn't remember the umbrella.

Not even the wet spot inside the doorway of her house where some rain had spattered in reminded her. She ran up the stairs and there her grandmother was . . . still sitting on the straight chair in the middle of the room and facing the door.

"Grandmother!" said Kim joyously. "I have two wonderful books. I will tell you the stories in them as I read them. You liked *Shen of the Sea*. Remember? The funny stories? The one about tea? And—"

"Where is the umbrella?" Grandmother asked in Chinese. "Bam Boo Shoot!"

"O-o-oh!" gasped Kim.

She put her books on the floor in the corner where the umbrella had been standing as though they were a token, a promise to the room, to the corner, but especially to Grandmother, that the umbrella would soon be back.

"I'll get it! I'll get it! I know where it is! I'll be right back with it," she cried.

Kim tore down the stairs two at a time. She flew. She tore around the corner . . . never mind puddles and falling into sky clouds! She tore into the library and up the stairs to the Children's Room. There was the rack! But it was empty.

The big, black umbrella was gone!

3

Grandmother

"O-O-OH!" GASPED KIM. "MY UMBRELLA! MY FATHER'S UMBRELLA!"

She looked wildly around. She saw Mrs. Parks at her desk in the mending room and she rushed in there. The big boy who had been mending books had gone. Mrs. Parks was alone. She jumped up from her swivel chair and ran to Kim.

"What's the matter, Kim?" she asked. "Whatever is the matter?"

Tears, heavy as the rain, began to pour down Kim's cheeks.

"My umbrella!" she wailed. "My father's big black umbrella! It's gone!" She grabbed Mrs. Parks by the arm and pulled her to the umbrella rack. "There! You see? I left it right there . . . in that corner square. I forgot it. I forgot it when I went home. I came right back! But it's gone!"

Kim bent over the rack and tapped the square, the very square in the back left-hand corner where she had carefully stood the umbrella. "Folded tightly," she said, "snapped together tightly, neatly . . ."

Kim looked down into the rack as if the umbrella, besides having a secret place in its handle, might also be a magic one that could shrink itself, if it wanted to, into a tiny umbrella, fool her . . . and then stretch and stretch itself way way up again, even out of the rack altogether, it might get to be so big!

Big or little, magic or not, it just was not in the rack. Kim rushed around the room, here and there, with the library teacher trying to catch up with her. But no one there had the umbrella . . . you couldn't hide anything that big. They went downstairs to the big people's library and looked. A library teacher down there said that Kim could have a pretty flowered umbrella that was in the cloak room. Someone had left it in the library a long long time ago and had never come back for it . . . Kim could have that.

Kim shook her head. How could that umbrella take the place of her father's special umbrella?

Now Kim could not control her sobs.

"Oh, Kim!" the library teacher said. "I'm so sorry. Oh, dear! But . . . maybe the person who took the umbrella will bring it back . . . when he sees it is not his . . . maybe he just didn't want to get wet and will bring it back . . . there are honest people in the world . . ."

But Kim Chu sobbed on. "My grandmother will slap me," she said.

"Kim," the library teacher said, "tell your grandmother what happened . . . that somebody took the umbrella . . . by mistake, maybe . . . and will bring it back . . . maybe . . ."

Kim looked doubtful. But she went home. Rapidly, in a torrent of Chinese, she explained all these things to her grandmother and her grandmother did slap her. She reminded Kim that she had warned her not to take the umbrella, but Kim had taken it anyway. Now, Kim must go out again and look everywhere . . . all over Chinatown . . . everywhere . . . for that umbrella.

Kim went back to the library. She didn't know what else to do. Maybe the library teacher was right, maybe the person had brought the umbrella back. Maybe that person's grandmother had said, "That is not your umbrella! Take it right back to the library!" And had given that person a slap.

But nobody had returned it.

The library teacher put her arm around Kim. "There now, Kim," she said. "I know what I'll do . . . make a big sign and tie it to the umbrella rack . . . I'll do it this minute. Come on!"

They went into the mending room and the teacher printed a sign in big black letters on a strong piece of cardboard. The sign said:

WILL THE PERSON WHO TOOK THE BIG BLACK UMBRELLA PLEASE
BRING IT BACK. IT BELONGS TO MR. LIN CHU.

She tied the sign to the front of the rack and all the children in the room crowded around trying to find out what was going to happen . . . a special story hour, perhaps?

Mrs. Parks explained. "The umbrella that is lost is the umbrella of Mr. Lin Chu," she said gravely. "I hope it will be returned."

"O-o-oh! Mr. Chu-u-u!" the children echoed and one boy whistled.

Everyone in Chinatown knows practically everyone else, and

some may even have remembered about the secret of the bamboo handle, for the story of it had gotten into some newspapers.

Just then a little girl tore up the stairs and pushed through the gathering around the umbrella rack. It was Mae Lee, Kim's best friend at Chinese School!

"Kim! What's the matter, Kim?" she asked breathlessly.

Between sobs, Kim explained.

"O-o-oh! My!" exclaimed Mae Lee, for she knew the secret of the bamboo handle. She and her whole family had been at the dinner party when the umbrella was presented to Mr. Chu. "That is ter-rible," she said. "I wish I could help you find it . . . But, I have to hurry, or I'll miss my train and my ferry! I'm late already."

She plunked her books on the desk, said she didn't have time to pick out new ones today . . . she was so late. "See you Monday!" she said to Kim. "That thief better return your father's umbrella, he better . . . or . . . Well, I'll keep my eyes peeled!"

She gave Kim Chu a meaningful look of the eyes, a shrug of the shoulders, and a frown on the forehead. Then she sped down the stairs.

Kim hated to see her go. But somehow she felt a little hopeful . . . first, the big sign on the umbrella rack, and then her best friend rushing into the library at that very minute, giving her the nod, the meaningful signals with her eyes and her shoulders, that they both practiced for when they got to be actresses.

Kim stopped crying and went home again. But when she got there she climbed the stairs slowly, slowly, as slowly as ancient Mr. Wu who lived in the front rooms, looking out at the El. She explained everything to Grandmother. But Grandmother slapped her again. She said that signs on racks were not enough, that Kim must search more carefully, everywhere . . . for that umbrella. "Go!" she said.

Kim went out. She went back to the library again. It was as though she couldn't believe that the umbrella was really lost. The dragon on the scroll in it might be a magic one and had spirited away the umbrella for a little jaunt. Now, maybe it would be back. It wasn't. Mrs. Parks said that she would go home with Kim and explain everything to Kim's grandmother, tell her that sometimes things do get returned . . . that all the children who were in the library had promised to be on the lookout.

"Is there a reward?" asked one tall girl, the last child to leave the Children's Room which was soon to close.

"Oh, yes!" promised Kim, her eyes big.

Mrs. Parks went home with Kim. While the library teacher explained all that had happened to Grandmother, with Kim putting the explanation into Chinese, Grandmother's expression did not change at all. The library teacher, about to leave, tried to shake hands with Grandmother. But Grandmother did not notice her outstretched hand.

Mrs. Parks gave Kim a gentle pat on her wet head. She said, "Tell me tomorrow how everything is." And she left.

Then Grandmother slapped Kim again. She said, "You must find the umbrella. And don't bring home any more teachers instead!"

Kim Chu went out again. She did not go back to the library. She did not walk up and down the streets of Chinatown either, looking for someone with a big umbrella like her father's, because it looked exactly like most other big, black ones. The only way she could tell her father's umbrella was to ask to examine the handle. And she was afraid to do that.

Kim felt worse than ever as she thought about the importance of her father's umbrella. She stood disconsolately at the foot of the stairs leading up to the elevated train station. She leaned against the post there, watching the people come down. She wished that her mother and father would come on the next train and she could tell them the awful thing that she had done. Her father would tell the mayor . . . maybe the mayor would know how to find the umbrella . . . or maybe make a new scroll for another secret handle of another umbrella . . .

That would not be the same, though. And slow tears trickled down Kim's cheeks again. It was too early for her mother and father to be coming home and to pick up little Shoo-Shoo at her aunt's house.

But Kim resolved to wait for them here.

4

The Three Nickels

KIM LOOKED UP AT THE LIVELY ELEVATED STATION. TRAINS KEPT COM-
ing in and going out. At this time of day there were a great many of
them. Hardly would one leave the station when another would come
roaring in, making the platform above quiver and shake. And down
below, the pillar that Kim was leaning against vibrated and made her
arms and shoulders tingle.

Two trains rattled into the station at the same time, one going
uptown, the other downtown. Many people hurried down the stairs,
impatient with the slow ones, getting around them as best they could,
anxious to get home and have dinner.

Kim stood aside, so as not to get pushed out of the way or
knocked down. When everybody had left, and the two trains had
rattled along the tracks, she leaned against her pillar again. Should
she wait for her mother and father? Or . . . should she go home?

Maybe Grandmother would not slap her again. She'd go home.

About to leave, she spotted a nickel on the bottom step. She picked it up. It was an old-timer nickel, a buffalo nickel. And there! On the next step up . . . there was another nickel! It, also, was a buffalo nickel. Now she had two nickels. Perhaps there would be a nickel on every single step that led to the top. There wasn't a nickel on the next step, but on the fifth step up, there was another nickel! It, too, was a buffalo nickel.

"Raining buffalo nickels," thought Kim. She put the nickels in her pocket, and feeling happier now, she went up and up and up, carefully scrutinizing every step. She even poked under chewing gum wrappers in the corners thinking a buffalo nickel might be hidden beneath. It was as though the nickels she had found were saying, "Follow us!" Like the crumbs on the forest floor that were supposed to guide Hansel and Gretel through the woods, these nickels might be supposed to guide her to her father's lost umbrella.

"Someone must have a hole in his pocket, dropping nice nickels like this, not noticing, in a hurry like everybody else," she thought. "A person might have dropped them some time ago and nobody noticed them, . . . 'til now, 'til me!"

Looking for more lost nickels had led Kim now to the topmost platform of the station where the Third Avenue El ran. She had never been up here before. In one direction she could see Mott Street with its pretty, bright little shops. Chinatown looked tiny from up here, and so busy! In the other direction she could see the library with its lights lighted at the entrance. It looked tiny, too. Then she looked down Park Row. She figured out which house was hers. How far away everything seemed! It was as though she didn't live here.

Kim jingled the three nickels in her pocket.

A sign in the window of a little booth said, FARE, 5 CENTS. "You probably give your nickel in at that window," Kim thought, "to ride on the elevated train."

She had never ridden on an El train. Her heart pounded with excitement. The three nickels must be telling her to get on a train, herself . . . the next train.

She went up to the booth and shoved one of her nickels through the rounded opening of the glass partition to a man who was reading a newspaper. The man scowled at the nickel, shoved it back to Kim, and gestured her away impatiently.

"Oh," thought Kim. "You must pay on the train, like we did that time on the trolley car. What a dumbbell he must think I am!" She looked back at him to see if he thought she was a dumbbell, but he was reading his paper again.

"I'm not a dumbbell," she reassured herself. "I got 'A' in geography."

Then Kim went over to the gate where you were supposed to get onto the platform where the trains ran. The gate was a turnstile, but it wouldn't turn. And a train was coming, roaring in, shaking the platform even worse when you were standing on it than it had seemed to do from below.

Kim felt she had to catch this train and do what the nickels were telling her. Quick as a flash, she got down on her stomach and squeezed under the turnstile. She picked herself up. She was on the shaking, vibrating platform and the train was coming at a mile a minute. Was it going to stop? Could it?

Kim felt frightened. But she held up her hand, the way people do to buses to make them stop. And the train did stop with a sudden, shuddering screech; and a door opened right in front of Kim.

People! She had to duck over to one side of the door to get out of their way. They poured out of this door and out of all the doors up and down the platform, pushing, shoving, in a terrible hurry to get somewhere. They all looked cross. Then a few people who were standing on the platform, rushed to the door to get onto the train, and they almost knocked Kim down. But she managed to get on the

train, too, just in the nick of time! For the door closed like magic behind her so fast it was a wonder her red coat didn't get caught in it.

Goodness! People do this every day, thought Kim. My! Her own mother and father did this every day. Oh, my! What brave people!

She got away from the door and went into a long car. There were not very many people left on the train. She found a good seat in a little area where two that were straw-covered faced one another. No one else was sitting in here, it was like her own little house, and she sat by the window where she could look out.

She felt very happy now. She had two buffalo nickels in her coat pocket and the other one in her moist palm to give the conductor when he came around. But he never came. "You must pay when you get off," she reasoned. And she decided to enjoy the ride, her first on an elevated train.

"I'm going to the land of the lost umbrellas," she thought happily. "The nickels are taking me there. I must keep my eyes peeled . . . like Mae Lee. Wherever she is now, she is keeping her eyes peeled, too, for my father's umbrella."

As the train went ricketty-rocketty along the tracks, Kim looked out of her window and into the windows of the tenements along Park Row. She could see into people's room, see what some people were doing. "It's like a moving picture," she thought.

An old man was leaning on a pillow on his windowsill and he was looking out. He mainly watched what was going on in the street below, perhaps to say hello to someone he knew. In his other window a big dog was lolling on the sill, its front paws hanging over the ledge. It was watching the train and its head turned from right to left and left to right as the train roared down the track. The dog looked happy

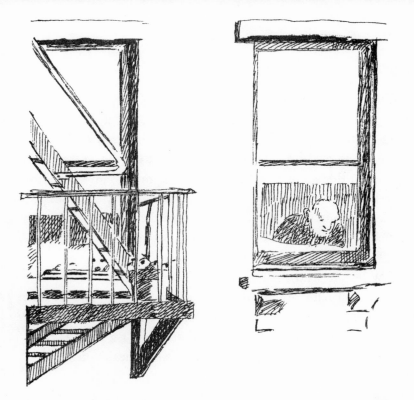

with its long pink tongue rolling out of the side of its mouth. Kim looked back and waved to him as she sped by.

"What a wonderful ride!" she thought.

Suddenly, just then, a conductor came through Kim's car. She had her nickel ready for him. But he wasn't taking up nickels. He was shouting something. Kim didn't have any idea what he was shouting . . . maybe it was not in English . . . or Chinese.

"SOUFERYLASTOPEVVVYBAEEOFF!"

That's what he said. All one word. Kim watched him. He went to the front of the car and he wound up a sign high in the window there. She hadn't even noticed it. Some eye-peeler, she was, she thought, disgusted with herself.

The sign said SOUTH FERRY, and the conductor wound it until it said 168th St. Now, she understood. South Ferry was where this train was going. And he was telling everybody to get off the train when it got there. And she hadn't seen one single sign of the lost umbrella yet! The conductor picked up some newspapers from the seats and the floor and then he went through to the next car slamming the door behind him and shouting the same strange word in there. Only now, Kim understood the word.

The few people who were in Kim's car got up and went to stand at the door. So did Kim. Again the train stopped with a shudder and a lurch. Kim almost fell down, but she caught herself. Then everybody pushed off in a hurry, even though there wasn't a crowd. Now they were on a platform and from here you could hear a deep, long *Too-oot! Too-oot!*

People from all the cars of the elevated rushed, pushed, shoved ahead to where the toots were coming from, and these toots were sounding louder and louder and more and more urgent. Kim rushed, too. She had to rush or else be knocked down by some big rusher. She didn't know where they were rushing. She couldn't see one thing. People crowded around her, all bigger than she was. The next thing she knew she was at a booth where the rushers pushed coins through the window.

The booth was too high for Kim to reach, and a lady behind her said, "Hurry up, little girl, or we'll miss it!"

The lady pushed Kim ahead of her and across a metal ramp and onto a wooden platform that was slightly rocking. "Why!" thought Kim. "I am on a boat . . . a ferryboat, that's where the elevated train and the nickels have brought me! Now, what?"

"We'll get my favorite seat," said the lady. She was a jolly lady for she was chuckling about something. Maybe just getting the good seat. She pushed Kim toward a long, highly polished wooden seat that spread along the back of the ferry on the open deck. It was sheltered from the wind by the cabin behind it. The wide door to the cabin was open and some people went in there. But Kim and the laughing lady were sitting where they could see the ferry slip and the city. Kim saw the elevated tracks, too, and even the train, still resting there, that she had just gotten off.

The ferryboat sounded three more long drawn out *too-oots*. Some people leaned on the railings, others strolled around. Everybody on the boat looked happy. Kim felt happy, too. "Who wouldn't be happy being on a boat?" she thought.

Now the engines were starting up and the floor under Kim's feet vibrated. Her toes in her wet shoes felt tingly, and she wiggled them as though they had been asleep.

Then a man in a yellow raincoat who was standing at the back of the boat unhooked a heavy, weather-beaten, shaggy rope, dragged it across the deck and hooked it up on the other side.

"That rope means—nobody else get on or get off," thought Kim almost bursting with excitement; for now the trip was about to begin.

The man at the rope blew sharply on a whistle, the ferryboat sounded another wonderful, bonging *too-oot* and the engines, going harder now, made the waters churn.

The lady next to Kim chuckled again. Kim didn't know what the lady was laughing about. She shyly looked around so she could see what the joke might be, for she did not want to appear stupid on her first ferry ride.

"Will you just look at that!" said the lady. And then Kim saw what probably was making the lady laugh.

For suddenly, as the ferry began to edge out of the slip, a tall man rushed for the boat. You could see him racing licketty-cut across the wharf, bellowing as he came, "Wait! Wait!" and brandishing what seemed to be a cane, held like a sword before him.

There was already a small gap between the boat and the wharf. But the man at the rope leaned out his long, strong arm, grabbed the tall, running man by his arm, and pulled him over the gap, not an easy thing to do, for the man almost tripped on his . . . cane . . . but he made it! He was on!

Some people clapped, some said, "Hooray!" Most people paid little attention. But the lady next to Kim laughed harder than ever. She shook with delight and slapped her knees.

"That's Go-getter Terwilliger for you!" she said. "Always gets what he goes after. Wanted this ferry. Got it! Isn't that right, little girl? Go-getter Terwilliger gets everything he goes after." She talked as though she thought Kim was bound to know all about Go-getter Terwilliger. So Kim gave a little "Heh-heh!" as though she did.

The man was panting and seemed somewhat confused. He stood for a moment in front of Kim and the laughing lady but he did not notice them. He mopped his brow. He was looking around for a place to sit. Then he saw a good seat. It was at the railing on the long,

curved bench that wound around the boat to the left of where Kim and the jolly lady were sitting. The man had on a dark suit . . . but it looked damp. So did his black hat.

"Probably got caught in the rain, poor man, like me," Kim thought.

He looked like a millionaire man, or a mayor, dressed in such fine clothes and carrying a cane like that. He put his cane between his knees . . . Oh! It wasn't a cane. Naturally, on a day like this . . . it would be . . . it *was* an umbrella . . . a big, black umbrella neatly rolled up and clasped together.

His umbrella had a bamboo handle!

5

The Millionaire Man

KIM'S HEART THUMPED. WITHOUT SEEMING TO, SHE HAD TO KEEP HER eyes peeled on the millionaire man and his umbrella. There are lots of umbrellas like his, she assured herself. Still, why was he clutching this one so tightly between his knees, as though he were afraid it would get away? He didn't look very comfortable. He must think very highly of his umbrella. He must think it was a very important one, a rare one.

A rare umbrella like her father's. The idea took root in Kim's mind that the umbrella the millionaire man was clutching so tightly *was* her father's. Why else had the buffalo nickels led her first onto an elevated train and then onto a ferryboat? To bring her to this very spot at this very time. To bring her to her father's umbrella so she could recover it, put it back in the corner where it belonged, and so Grandmother would smile, not slap her again.

The time had come in real life when she must put into practice what she and Mae Lee had learned on the stage of the Chinese School.

If only Mae Lee were with her now! Two watchers are twice as good as one. She knew that Mae took an elevated train and a ferry to get home. Wouldn't it be funny if she were somewhere right here on this boat? She couldn't be, though, for she had left the library a long time ago. Still, Kim would have gone looking for her if she hadn't had to watch this man and his umbrella every minute.

Right now the man was putting on his eyeglasses. They were the kind that are only half-glasses, nothing up top, just glasses on the bottom half. Then he stood the umbrella up before him and gave it a little twirl on its tip, like a top. He tilted his head back and studied the umbrella through his half glasses. A slow smile spread over his face. And then he put the umbrella back in its tight place between his knees.

He then adjusted his eyeglasses. It was hard to know where he was looking with that kind of eyeglasses. They might be especially created for the purpose of watching people. He might be watching *her*, now, just as hard as she was watching him. He might be able to see through her and to have seen the idea pop into her head that his umbrella was the lost umbrella of her father. She must be careful . . . watch him only out of the corners of her eyes. It was lucky he was sitting so close with no one in between.

Now the man got a newspaper out of his pocket. It looked soggy. He must have bought it before he had his big umbrella. His coat looked wet, too, as wet as Kim's own. He looked as though he'd had quite a drenching! So, he could not have had his umbrella for very long!

38

Oh! Suddenly Kim remembered a sopping wet man who had pushed past her to get into the library and out of the rain. Was this the same man? She had not taken in what he looked like, only that he was tall. Could this be the very same man? Could he have spotted her fine, big, man's umbrella as she was strolling along under it, happily, in the rain?

Could he have stolen it?

The man opened up his newspaper. He gave it a little punch to stay open. The name of his soggy paper was *The Wall Street Journal*. At first he didn't seem to know whether to hold his newspaper in front or behind the umbrella. He tried it both ways. At last he decided to hold it inside of the umbrella. This was good for Kim. She could keep her eyes on the whole umbrella. For had the handle of the umbrella been hidden by the newspaper, how could she tell whether or not the man was studying it and figuring out how to unscrew it?

For if this umbrella the millionaire man was guarding so closely was really her father's, then this man must know the secret of the bamboo handle. He must have read about it in the newspapers. In one of the papers there had even been a picture of the New Year's dragon. You couldn't see her father because he was in the dragon's head. But you could see his dancing feet. "These are my father's feet," Kim had proudly told her friends. The paper told about the special umbrella that had been awarded to her father as a prize for his dragon design. The paper even described the secret of the handle.

When this man read that story he must have said to himself, "H-m-m! Some umbrella! I'd like to get hold of that!"

And today, this very rainy day, his chance had come! He'd probably been on the watch for it every rainy day. Now he had it!

"Go-getter Terwilliger!" That's what the lady called him.

Kim grew angry. Why, a man like this could buy one hundred umbrellas if he wanted to. But perhaps he was a collector of umbrellas, rare ones, and wanted this one so badly that he would steal up the stairs of the library to the Children's Room and snatch her umbrella from the rack, the back square on the left. And no one to see him and shout, "Stop thief!" And all the while she and Mrs. Parks were looking for funny books!

"Go-getter Terwilliger!" The jolly lady was muttering the name to herself and shaking with laughter again. She must know the millionaire man. Maybe once, together, on the ferryboat they had read about the dragon story and were talking about it and she had said, "There, now, there's an umbrella for you, Mr. Go-getter. Try to get hold of that one!" That's what she might have said then.

Out of the blue, suddenly, "Yessiree!" said the lady right now,

with a deep chuckle. "Have to hand it to Go-getter!"

Kim took her eyes off the millionaire man and looked at the laughing lady who was on her right. She looked nice. Between chuckles she took in deep, long breaths of the pure sea air. She loved being on the boat. Maybe she would be a friend and help Kim get her umbrella back? Before the boat got to where it was going.

Kim knew she was on a ferryboat like those she and her family had seen that time long ago from Brooklyn Bridge, but she didn't know where it was going.

Should she ask the lady? Yes, she answered herself.

She said, "Mrs. Lady. Excuse me. Where is this boat going?"

The lady took a pair of half glasses, just like Mr. Go-getter's, out of her pocketbook, put them on, looked over the no-glass part at Kim and said, "Why, to St. George!"

"St. George!" exclaimed Kim.

"Why, yes," said the lady. "St. George! Are you lost?"

"No . . . no!" said Kim. She tried to laugh. "Hah! I'm not lost. I'm here."

"I see," said the lady, and she chuckled. "A good answer, indeed!"

Then the lady got a book out of her big carpetbag, opened it to a page she had a bookmark in and started, or seemed to start, to read. She made a happy chuckling sound. It must be a funny book she was reading.

But Kim was worried. "St. George," she said to herself. She knew the story of St. George and the Dragon. They had read it in school. The millionaire man probably knew the story, too. He might be going to a secret meeting somewhere in St. George where they were going to act out the story. When he showed them her father's umbrella with

41

the dragon scroll in it they might let him be St. George in the play
. . . the best part.

Before the lady could get deep into her funny book, Kim said,
"Excuse me, please, Mrs. Lady. But, what does this boat do when it
gets to St. George."

"Goes back," said the lady. "Goes back to the Battery again.
That's what it does . . . it goes back. And with me on it, too. I ride
back and I ride forth. I ride back and forth. But you! Are you sure
you are not lost?"

"Ho-ho, no!" said Kim. She managed to give a little chuckle
herself. "I'm right here! Brooklyn Bridge is over there. The blimp, the
Goodyear blimp is in the sky . . . I see it often from my roof. The
Statue of Liberty is over there. And, you are here. So . . . I am not
lost."

The lady laughed and thwacked her knee with glee. "Good answer! Good answer, indeed!" she said again. Then she added, "And
. . . Go-getter is there!"

"Go-getter, yes," said Kim hesitantly.

The lady then began to read, or seemed to. Kim was worried. She
decided that this lady was a smart lady. All along she might have been
watching Kim, had put on her half-glasses to watch better and not to
read. Had she . . . could she have . . . suspected that the umbrella
her friend, Go-getter Terwilliger, was clutching, was Kim's own
father's? This lady who seemed so jolly, so friendly, might have be-
gun to think something.

The millionaire man was very smart, too. Creeping up library
stairs like that . . . stealing a rare umbrella, pretending to read a
newspaper now, before Kim Chu, the real right owner of this um-

42

brella who was sitting just seven feet away, could get it back. If it was her umbrella! *Ts!*

How to outwit two grown-up, smart people like these and get her umbrella back, Kim wondered in despair.

Then, suddenly, a little girl appeared from around the bend of the boat on the side where the millionaire man was sitting. It was Mae Lee!

She stopped as though to watch a screaming gull. Then, leaning nonchalantly against the railing beside the millionaire man, she turned and looked at Kim Chu.

Kim was almost exploding with joy. Mae Lee! Her best friend in Chinese School, her acting partner in plays, the very best actress in Chinese School, grades four to six! Mae Lee had promised to keep her eyes peeled for Kim's father's umbrella, and she had.

Mae Lee slowly moved her head back and forth and looked at Kim with a deep, meaningful stare. She carelessly pressed a finger on her lips as though to wipe away a crumb. But Kim knew this meant, "DON'T LET ON THAT WE KNOW EACH OTHER!"

Kim looked up at the blimp. But her heart was hammering with excitement. For now, two little girls had their eyes peeled on the big, black umbrella and the man who was clutching it. He could not possibly escape!

6

Mae Lee

WITH THE ARRIVAL OF MAE LEE, KIM'S SPIRITS BOUNCED SKY HIGH. A wide smile spread over her face. Now things would begin to happen. Now the two of them would work together to get Kim's umbrella back from the millionaire man. It was not going to be easy, the way he was hanging onto it. But she and Mae together would carry it off . . . somehow.

For a few minutes Mae Lee leaned against the railing with her elbows stretched out behind her. She let her eyes fall now and then on the big, black umbrella, carelessly, as though she wasn't really *looking* at it, as though her mind was on anything else but it.

Then, with her hands clasped lightly behind her, she strolled across the deck in front of Kim and the jolly lady to the other side of the boat. Before rounding the bend on that side, she looked back at Kim. After a slight nod of her head, a hitch of her right shoulder, and a long impenetrable stare that meant, "Follow me!" she disappeared around the bend.

Kim stood up, stretched, and then she too strolled to that side of the boat. Mae was waiting for her by the railing. No one was sitting nearby, so no one would get the idea that something was up or overhear the conversation.

Still Kim and Mae took special care with the way they spoke to one another. They spoke out of the sides of their mouths—lips opened just a crack at the corners—a way they had often practiced at school. Sometimes an "s" sounded like a "z." It sounded curious, like another language or a code, and this was bound to throw an eavesdropper off, if one came by.

Mae Lee muttered, "You know what happened? This. I left the library the minute the library lady put up the sign. I wanted to help find your umbrella. But I had to hurry to catch the El and make my boat. I was late already. I tore up the stairs to the El because I heard a train coming . . . and . . . I made it!"

"Train . . . yes . . ." said Kim breathlessly as though she herself had just run up those El stairs.

Mae went on. "Now listen to this, will you? As the door of the train slammed shut behind me, that man sitting near you on the boat, that man in that wet, dark suit, hanging onto that umbrella with the bamboo handle, we-ell! that man rushed onto the platform and dropped his nickel in. But . . . he was too late! 'Hold it! Hold it!' he bellowed, seeing that the next door to mine was still open. But that door slammed in his face, too. Was he mad! He shook the umbrella after the train as we got going. If I could have gotten off the train right then I would have, and I would've followed the crook, kept my eyes peeled on him. Because I do think he *is* the crook . . . best-dressed people are often crooks I read somewhere. But the door was closed. And I was in, and he was out!"

"O-o-h!" gasped Kim. "He must know the secret of the handle . . ."

"Exactly what I thought!" said Mae. "It just flashed into my mind that the umbrella he waved at the train was your father's. You couldn't help but see how wet he was. Why would a man who was carrying an umbrella that big get to be so wet? Just got hold of it, I said to myself. So-o-o . . ."

"So-o-o," repeated Kim impatiently.

Mae continued. "At the very next station I got off my train and waited for the next train. I figured that the mad, wet man would be on it and so I'd get on it, too . . . I'd already missed my regular boat anyway, I figured. I had to keep my eyes on him and that umbrella if I could."

"So . . . what happened then?" asked Kim forgetting to speak code.

"Sh-sh-sh!" said Mae. "Careful how you speak . . . may be spies in the cabin. Well, it all happened as I thought. From the platform where I was standing I could see into the cars of the next train when it slowed up. Sure enough! There was that man sitting by the window in the second car. I got on. I sat down right opposite him and I looked, without his knowing it, long and fast at the umbrella, wondering how to get it for you."

Kim's eyes brimmed with tears at the thought of such kindness. Her friend missing boats and everything for her father's umbrella!

Mae went on. "That man was probably wondering how the

46

girl . . . me . . . that he'd seen in the window of the train he'd missed was now here on this train, sitting right opposite him. Maybe he thought I had seen him steal the umbrella? Because, as we neared South Ferry Station, that's when he began to clutch the umbrella between his knees the way he's doing now . . ."

Kim was puzzled. "If you and the man were on the same El, why did he have to run to catch the ferry and jump over the rope? You didn't."

"He just stayed behind on purpose, hid . . . trying to give me the slip, till he saw I was on the boat and had probably gone to the front . . . you know how kids do . . . they run to the front where it's more fun. Then when I was out of sight he tore for the boat. Oh! I saw it all, from the cabin . . . and I heard the cheers!"

"I hope he's scared, seeing you standing right beside him, after all. I hope he's trembling. I am. To think we have to catch a thief . . . such a big one! A millionaire man thief! Wow!"

"Well . . . we have to, we have to," said Mae with a shrug. "But what I want to know is how *you* happen to be on my ferry. Was I surprised to see you get onto my boat! I almost said 'Hello.'"

Kim explained about the buffalo nickels and she showed them to Mae.

"H-m-m," said Mae. "Well-ll . . ." It was clear the nickels were an unexpected thing for her to have to ponder and she frowned as she pondered. Then she shrugged. "Well," she said, "we must get back to work. I'll go the long way around and stand by the man, and you go back to your seat by the laughing lady."

"You've noticed how much she laughs?" said Kim.

"Yes," said Mae. "I notice everything."

47

"She knows that man. She calls him Go-getter Terwilliger," said Kim.

"She does?" mused Mae. "Maybe they're in cahoots," she said.

Kim sighed. "But she does seem so nice! I hope she's not in cahoots," she said. She began to tremble. "We're surrounded by crooks!" she murmured awe-stricken.

"Don't shake!" said Mae. "This place will be our meeting place to say what we think or have found out . . . We report right here!" Mae smacked the railing with her hand.

'Yes," said Kim. "And I'm not trembling now. See?" And she slapped the railing too.

"All right," said Mae. "We have about fifteen minutes before the ferry reaches Saint George . . ."

"I always thought you lived on Staten Island," said Kim.

"Same thing. Saint George is part of Staten Island. It's where the ferry lands."

"Dragons there?" asked Kim.

"Who knows?" said Mae. "Who knows?"

"The man might want to play the part of St. George and they might let him do it if she shows them the scroll," said Kim.

"Possible. Possible," said Mae wisely. "Anyway, we have to work fast. I'm off. Pretend you never laid eyes on me before in your life. We must bamboozle them."

Mae Lee strolled away, hands clasped carelessly behind her, and she disappeared around the bend at the front of the ferry.

"What a brave girl." Kim sighed. "She probably never trembles." Then, swaying slightly, her hands also clasped carelessly behind her, Kim sauntered back to her seat beside the lady, who was shaking with laughter again.

It was hard to think that such a jolly lady could be in cahoots with a crook. It just must be that the book she was reading *was* an awfully funny one, Kim thought. She looked at the name of the book —*War and Peace*. It didn't sound funny. The lady had her finger on line five of page forty-nine, not to lose her place while chuckling.

The man was still sitting there, clutching the umbrella and reading his newspaper or pretending to. Then Mae Lee came strolling along and resumed her watching position at the railing. She rocked back and forth on her feet from heel to toe and glanced around sometimes, as though bemused by the sights, but she took it in that the man was still on page two of his newspaper. Still, she could understand his not making swifter progress for the print was very fine.

Then, suddenly, the man began to rock back and forth on *his* feet although he was still sitting down. Both Kim and Mae noticed this and gave one another the "on guard" stare. Had the man's feet gone to sleep and was he trying to wake them up for a stroll around the deck himself? If so, should they follow him? Although they were not yet near shore, perhaps he had decided to go to the rope so he could hop over, be the first one off and streak up the hill with his stolen umbrella. Could they catch such a long-legged man?

Mae signaled Kim to meet her at the railing and they both lost no time getting there.

"He's waking his feet up," said Mae.

"To make a quick getaway," said Kim.

"Yes, I thought the same thing. Listen, Kim," said Mae solemnly. "We are nearer the Staten Island side than the city. We haven't much time left . . ."

"O-o-h, dear," wailed Kim. She wished the ride could last forever so she would not have to go up to that millionaire man and say, "Give me back my father's umbrella." "Maybe it's not my father's umbrella after all?" she said, losing faith.

"Oh, it's his all right," said Mae reassuringly.

"How am I going to get it away from Go-getter Terwilliger?" asked Kim desperately.

"Good question," said Mae calmly. "Don't worry. We'll think of something . . . people always do."

"Maybe I should ask the jolly lady to help us," said Kim. "But she's reading . . . I don't like to bother her . . ."

"She's only pretending to read, and he is pretending. They stay on the same pages. That proves it . . . that they're in cahoots. They're watching us the way we're watching them. That's what tickles the lady's funny bone. Very funny!" she sneered. "But don't let on in any way that *we* know that *they* know we are watching them."

Kim was close to tears. Here the umbrella was, so close to her. How to get it? Oh, how to get it? Then two tears rolled down her cheeks. Hoping that Mae had not noticed, she reached in her pocket for her handkerchief. Instead, she felt the buffalo nickels that had led her here in the first place. They gave her courage. And so did Mae.

Mae said, "Have courage, friend. The moment is coming when we will have to know what to do. It must! Don't forget . . . creeping upstairs to the Children's Room, stealing . . . That's worse than if it had been down where the big people are . . ."

Now Kim Chu grew very angry. Her black eyes flashed. She tossed the tears off her cheeks. "He knows the secret . . . he knows the secret of the handle—knows that in the whole wide world there is not another one like it. One of the seven wonders of the world . . . jus-t about! And we will get it back!"

"Yes!" said Mae, equally angry. "And in cahoots with a lady who thinks it's funny!" She spat into the sea to express her disgust. "But now, back to our positions. The idea must come to us before we reach that buoy ahead there!"

Kim looked at the buoy! "O-oooh!" she said, for it wasn't far away. And she turned to go back to her seat.

Around the bend now . . . well-ll! There, in her seat, the millionaire man was sitting and talking out of the corner of his mouth to the laughing lady. He was still clutching the umbrella tightly between his knees. Both their heads were behind *The Wall Street Journal!*

"In cahoots! They really are in cahoots!" thought Kim aghast. And she tore back after Mae Lee.

7

The Millionaire Man
and the Laughing Lady

KIM CAUGHT UP WITH MAE AS SHE WAS ROUNDING THE BEND AT THE front of the boat. "Wait, Mae!" she said. "Come back! News!"

At the meeting place she said, "Mae. They're sitting together now! He's in my seat!"

"In your seat?" repeated Mae Lee incredulously. "Shows they are in cahoots! The lady laughs all the time to throw you off the track . . . make you think what a nice jolly lady she is. But all along she's been a partner of the man and . . . she must know the secret of the handle."

"Yes!" said Kim indignantly. "Asking me was I lost! Right this minute we should say to the two of them sitting in my seat. 'We know you have my father's umbrella! Give it back!'" Kim was so angry she could not help but speak loudly.

"Sh-sh-sh!" Mae Lee cautioned her and looked from left to right and behind them. But no one was around. "All right then," she said. "I'll go back my usual way and you go back yours. Then we, the two of us, will meet in front of them . . . the two of them. Two in cahoots against two in cahoots. That's fair!"

"We must hurry!" said Kim. "They must be thinking something . . . plotting something . . . they know we suspect them and they want to outwit us. But . . . Mae. When we get there, what will we say?"

"Say? Well . . . that will come to us, the right thing to say. And we will say it politely, nicely . . . Just say, 'We want that umbrella back! Come across!'"

Mae hurried off, not sauntering this time, on her regular beat around the boat.

Kim did not have as far to go as Mae. So she sauntered back to where the two were sitting. In her mind she rehearsed what she might say . . . just say . . . nicely . . . "There must be a mistake. But the nice man has my umbrella, my father's umbrella, and please give it back quietly . . . nicely . . ." She wouldn't say they'd call the police or anything to scare the man . . . or the jolly lady either, if she was in cahoots . . . Oh! But what a hard thing to do! she thought. As she rounded the bend she reminded herself of Mae's words: "Courage, my friend!"

But—around the bend now, all steeled to say what she had been thinking to say . . . and how to say it, like lines in a play, to the two of them together—she saw that the jolly lady was sitting alone again and that the millionaire man had gone back to his seat. Again he had the umbrella tightly clutched between his knees and had *The Wall Street Journal* spread out in front of him. Kim sat down in her seat next to the jolly lady who was having quite a fit of chuckling . . . her shoulders were shaking. She was staring at page forty-nine and her forefinger still marked the same place in line five.

Maybe Kim had imagined it all . . . that the man had been sitting in her seat just a few minutes before!

Then Mae Lee came. Pretending no surprise at finding the man back in his seat, she took up her usual position at the railing nearby, leaned on her elbows, and rocked on her feet, as usual. But a dark frown was on her face and her eyes flashed anger. Very soon she signaled Kim to join her at the meeting place. Once there, she said ominously, "They're trying to throw us off the track. They're stalling. They know we don't have many minutes left before the ferry docks. Anyway, one good thing . . . it's much easier to speak to one crook at a time. You speak! This minute. It's *your* father's umbrella, not my father's . . ."

"Supposing it isn't my father's umbrella anyway after all?" asked Kim. "Would I be arrested?"

"I'll come to see you in jail . . . bring you your homework and something to eat," Mae comforted her. "But I don't think you will be arrested . . . he's the one to be arrested," said Mae. "Racing up to the Chatham Square El Station, and all. You know . . . he probably saw me going into the library as he was coming out. And he probably thought *I* had seen *him* with your father's umbrella. Then . . . when he saw me on the elevated train, then he may have missed it on purpose . . . to give me the slip! But he didn't . . ." said Mae proudly. "We have him cornered!"

"Yes . . ." said Kim dolefully. "But I wish I'd already said, 'Give it back!' Come what, come may . . ."

"Courage, friend," said Mae. "We have to work fast now. You see that buoy bobbing in the ocean there? The minute we pass that buoy, the captain gives a toot. So people in Saint George can hurry down the hill and catch the boat going back to the city."

"O-o-oh!" gasped Kim and she hurried away. But as she rounded the bend, she stopped short. For there were the two sitting together again! Kim tore after Mae and this time the girls hurried through the cabin of the boat to the wide open door beside which, on the outside, on the deck, the two suspects were sitting, heads together as before behind *The Wall Street Journal*, plotting something . . . how to make their getaway with the stolen umbrella, probably, before the buoy bonged its somber tune.

The girls listened. The two of them were talking out of the side of their mouths to each other, but not in any code . . . in plain English. And they talked more loudly than Mae and Kim had talked at their meeting place. The girls could hear every single word the two were saying.

"George!" said the laughing lady.

"Yes, Daisy . . . yes?" said the millionaire man.

(Kim and Mae exchanged glances. This showed that the two were in cahoots for they knew each other by first names. So, why hadn't they tried to sit together? To throw Kim and Mae off . . . that's why . . .)

55

The lady said, "I knew you could carry it off, George. I just knew it. You're a winner, a born winner . . . you get everything you go after, George. 'Go-getter George!' You deserve the nickname. And this is so important! The most important thing you've set your sights on so far. You've carried it this far. Do you think you can carry it off?"

("O-o-ooh!" gasped Kim. "He'll probably leap over the rope . . . like when he got on . . ."

"Sh-sh-sh . . ." said Mae.)

"With you behind me, Daisy," said the man, "I can carry anything off!" Then he said, "Say, Daisy, by the way, have you noticed those two little girls . . . the one who stands behind me at the railing, and the other who sits beside you? One or the other of them has had her eyes on me the whole way over."

("Oh, we haven't," said Kim indignantly. "Sometimes we were at the meeting place."

"Anyway, we know how to watch so no one knows we are watching . . ." said Mae.)

The jolly lady chuckled. She could hardly talk she thought this was so funny. "Yes, George. I have noticed that . . ."

("I told you she was pretending to read," said Kim, "staying on page forty-nine!"

"Yes! And *The Wall Street Journal* . . . It's fine print, but you don't stay on page two forever!" said Mae.)

"George!" said Daisy. "What is there about you that is so special in the minds of these little girls?"

"I'm sure I don't know," said George with a shrug of his shoulders.

("Throwing us off," said Kim.)

"H-m-m," mused Daisy. She turned toward Go-getter George and peered at him through the top no-glass part of her glasses and then the glass part (the girls could see this through the window), and she said, "Nothing so very unusual about you . . . dressed nicely as always, carrying your umbrella neatly clasped together . . ."

("Throwing us off," said Mae.)

"There are probably a dozen or more men on this ferry boat, all nicely dressed, as you so charmingly put it, carrying umbrellas exactly like this one, neatly fastened together . . ." said Go-getter Terwilliger.

The lady mused. She said, "Well, George. I don't know . . . but there *is* something odd about the way you are holding your um-

57

brella, clutching it so tightly between your knees. And it's so wet!"

"Listen to me, Daisy!" said the man. "I have to clutch this umbrella. I have to hang onto it by hook or by crook. Because this umbrella . . ."

Kim and Mae were listening intently. But the word that came next was lost because, at that very moment, *"TOO-OOT! TOO-OOT!"* sounded the long, deep whistle of the ferryboat.

As though pressed by a button, passengers appeared from all sides, coming up from below and down from above. And true enough, exactly as the millionaire man had said, many men appeared and some of them had umbrellas that looked exactly like the one that the millionaire man was clutching.

The last thing Kim and Mae heard the man say was, "Well, nice talking to you, Daisy. I'm counting on you. But I have to hurry . . . Think I can carry this off?"

"Of course, George! Good luck!"

Kim gasped. "Hurry, Mae. We have to beat them to the front!"

"It's now or never!" said Mae.

They tore through the cabin and to the front of the boat as it began to bump and thrash its way into the slip. The man who was in charge of the heavy rope was already standing at the hook end. He was all set to unclasp the heavy hook the minute the boat docked. And that was to be right now!

Kim and Mae ran to the rope, ducking between people to get there. They stretched their arms straight out, fingers barely touching in the middle to give each other courage. And they needed it! For at this very moment the millionaire man, in a desperate hurry, rushed to the rope also.

"He wants to jump over again!" said Kim.

"Wait!" cried Mae Lee.

"Stop!" yelled Kim Chu. "There is a thief aboard!" She felt brave now that come what, come may was here. "An umbrella thief!" she and Mae cried out together. They could have made a wish had the time been suitable.

The rope man held his hand uncertainly on the heavy hook. But he did not unhook it. For the captain had sounded a special piercing whistle that meant, "HOLD EVERYTHING!"

And now the captain of the boat in his shiny blue suit and gold braid left his place at the helm and descended the little winding stairway. When he reached the deck he boomed, "What's all this about? What thief is on board this Staten Island ferry? Explain!" he said. "Explain!"

8

The Bamboo Handle

PEOPLE HAD ALREADY GATHERED AT THE ROPE TO HURRY OFF THE FERRY the minute it docked so they wouldn't miss the buses lined up on the wharf, already warming up to go. But everyone made way instantly for the captain, some on one side, some on the other. It was like the parting of the waters of the Red Sea in the Bible.

The captain stalked through this opening and stood at the rope where Kim Chu and Mae Lee were confronting the crowd. They were resolved that they would not get off this boat and that they would not let the millionaire man off either until they had examined the handle of the umbrella that he was clutching close to him, in his arms now.

The captain eyed the two girls. He frowned. He squinted his bright blue eyes as though to take them in better. He switched his pipe from one corner of his mouth to the other. For a second he said nothing.

Kim was frightened. She wondered, "Is the captain going to put a gangplank out and make me walk it?" She looked at Mae whose lips were pursed together but down at the corners. She gave Kim a lift of the right eyebrow. This seemed to Kim to mean, "Overboard."

In this silent moment all you could hear was the *whoo-oosh, whoo-oosh* of the waves lapping against the sides of the ferry. The sea gulls poised on top of the piles of the pier stopped their piercing screams also.

The captain spoke. "H-m-m-m!" he said. He cleared his throat, took his pipe out of his mouth, wiped it on the seat of his pants, put it in his breast pocket behind the gold braid. Then, "What's all this about?" he boomed. It was like the blast of a cannon and two gulls flew away screeching. "What were the words I heard? Something about a thief on board my boat, *The Tottin Hill?*"

"Yes, sir!" said Kim. It was hard to hear her words. It was a wonder people didn't hear her heart instead, the way it was pounding! She said, "My umbrella was stolen. I mean, my father's umbrella was stolen."

"Where is your father?" boomed the captain, peering to the right, to the left, and behind him as though to spot a father. "Let that father come forward and make the accusation!"

"He can't," said Kim miserably. "He's at work in the Far East Restaurant on 125th Street."

"Well!" bellowed the captain. "How in the name of Sam Hill did your father's umbrella get on my ship if you didn't bring it on?"

"A thief brought it on," said Kim. You could hardly hear her at all now.

"Well," said the captain more gently. "Where is this thief then?"

Kim paused . . . it was come what, come may, all right. Mae

came to her rescue. "We tracked him to this boat," she said. She spoke softly too. Plays are better than real, she thought in her mind.

"Tracked him to this boat, eh! Well!" Now the captain was booming again . . . his name was Captain Magee; it said so in gold letters on his cap. "Who on my boat stole your father's umbrella? Whom did you track here? Where is he, that thief, and where did he, or she, steal it, and how . . . with your father up in the restaurant and all?"

Kim Chu drew in a long breath. She was getting in deeper now, the time for sink or swim, come what, come may . . . Time to point her finger at the millionaire man in the back with the laughing lady at his side. Bravely she said, "We think, Mae and I think (Mae uplifted her chin, showing she *did* think the same and was standing by what her friend thought) that that nice millionaire man who's back there with that nice laughing lady stole my father's umbrella from the Children's Room of the library this afternoon in the rain!"

"O-o-oh!" Some of the people gasped.

"What does your father's umbrella look like?" asked the captain.

"It's . . ." said Kim breathlessly. "It's a big, black one! And it has a bamboo handle . . . the one the nice millionaire man is clutching . . ."

"I shall examine all big, black umbrellas with bamboo handles before anyone with umbrellas such as those leaves this ship! First," said the captain, "will that 'nice millionaire man' as you call him . . . why, *Mister* Terwilliger! . . . please step forward. And also," said the captain, who looked quite startled, for it was plain to see that Mr. Terwilliger was the one Kim named as the thief, "will all gentlemen with black umbrellas which have bamboo handles step forward likewise?"

With this the millionaire man stepped forward. Seven other men, all of whom had big, black umbrellas with bamboo handles, emerged from here and there in the crowd and made quite a semicircle around Kim Chu, Mae Lee and the captain. The laughing lady edged her way forward also.

One man with that sort of umbrella said, "I thought maybe I might be the 'nice millionaire man' in question." He gave a high giggle, thinking he was funny, and some people did laugh.

"This is not a time for jokes," said the captain sternly. "I have to settle this matter. People have to catch buses. Ferries must run on schedule. *The Tottin Hill* must dock. But first, since this little girl has made a serious charge—that there is a thief on my boat—that thief must be caught!"

People stopped laughing right away. They formed a semicircle around the accused . . . the 'nice millionaire man' and the seven other bamboo-handled umbrella-holders who had also stepped forward.

All the umbrellas looked exactly alike.

The millionaire man was a kind-looking man, and he was smiling gently. He looked the nicest of all the men, not at all like a crook who would go creeping up library stairs to steal a small child's father's umbrella. "The little girl must be wrong," some thought. "*Ts!* Children!"

The captain said to Kim, "What is your name, little girl?"

"Kim Chu. Fifty-nine Park Row," said Kim. "Age nine."

"All right, Kim. Step forward, please," said the captain. He wasn't booming any more, he was nice. Kim thought he would not make her walk the plank, come what, come may. The captain said, "There are seven men plus your 'millionaire man,' who makes eight, with eight identical umbrellas. Can you tell your father's from all the others?"

"Yes, sir," said Kim. "I can . . . fast . . . if I can hold them . . ."

"Very well," said the captain. "Umbrella men! Get in line! Step forward, one at a time. Let Kim Chu examine your umbrellas!"

One cross man said, "Me first. If I miss my bus I will be late for my meeting. Here, kid. Take a look. I got it for Father's Day."

Kim took the cross man's umbrella, quickly tried the handle and, as she expected, it did not untwist. She handed it back. "No," she said.

"That is not my father's."

That cross man leaped over the rope then and dashed off sputtering with indignation. "Children!"

The other umbrella men were more curious. They all seemed to know Mr. Terwilliger, the "nice millionaire man" at whom Kim had pointed her finger. Many of the other passengers besides the laughing lady seemed to know Mr. Terwilliger, and all were curious to see what was going to happen.

"Maybe he *is* a mayor, not a millionaire . . . maybe both," thought Kim as she swiftly examined umbrella after umbrella. Owners of these umbrellas did not hop over the rope and leave the ferry,

however. They were too curious and had liked being in line with Mr. Terwilliger.

One of the umbrella men, he was number five, said to Kim in a low voice, "I see you know what you are doing . . . I am a lawyer . . . if you need any advice . . . my name is Mr. Jack Dooly . . ."

He almost spoke the way Mae and Kim did, out of the side of his mouth, but he said his *s*'s. "Thank you, sir," said Kim. She handed him back his umbrella, for it was not her father's. Neither was the sixth man's nor the seventh man's. And now it was the millionaire man's turn!

There was a tense silence. Supposing the little girl was right? In the silence Kim heard a lady near the front say to the person next to her, "You know who that is . . . don't you? Terwilliger . . . 'Go-getter Terwilliger' . . . the Borough President . . . wants to be the next mayor, you know . . . campaigning all over, campaigning . . ."

Kim Chu trembled. Mae Lee sidled along the rope to stand closer to Kim. She gave Kim a deep and meaningful look of the eye and a reassuring lift of the left eyebrow in the direction of the millionaire man. She side-spoke the words, "Be brave . . . we know he's our thief . . . pretend it's a play."

The curious crowd tried to draw in closer. But the captain roared, "Stand back! Stand back!"

So now, only the captain, Kim Chu, Mae Lee and the millionaire man were standing in the semicircle. As Kim took the millionaire man's umbrella she did not look at him. If she had looked, since he was so nice, she might have been tempted to hand him back the umbrella and say, "Never mind." But she didn't look at him. She took the umbrella and stood it up in front of her. It was so tall the handle reached to her eyes. She gently touched the handle. A slow smile spread over her face. The handle felt familiar to her. Gently, slowly, she began to try to untwist it. Oh . . . supposing it wouldn't open! Even Mae Lee was scared and trembling for she was Kim's accomplice. But . . . never mind all that . . . jail and everything . . . for the handle began to unwind. Kim slowly turned it this way and that

way until . . . off it came in her hands! Kim handed Mae the handleless umbrella and she held its handle up for the captain, the millionaire man, and everybody to see.

Then, reaching inside the handle, she carefully removed the charming and delicate scroll. She held it up and all the people gasped. So did the millionaire man; and the laughing lady, coming close up to Kim, stopped her chuckling.

Kim carefully untied the fragile silken cord and unrolled the scroll. "It is in Chinese," she said. "But this is what it means . . . and she translated into English the words that were inscribed there honoring her father, Mr. Lin Chu.

Everybody was astonished and spoke to one another even though they were strangers. "Did you hear that?" Some people were embarrassed for the millionaire man. On the other hand, some were outraged. One lady said, and rather loudly, "I think I'll vote for the other fellow this go-round . . ."

"Sh-sh-sh!" commanded the captain. "You will have to explain, sir, how this umbrella, this rare umbrella of Mr. Lin Chu's, happens to be in your hands."

"Well . . ." said Mr. Terwilliger. "H-m-m . . ."

"Stalling," said the lady in front.

"Or," said the captain to Kim, "can you give an explanation, Kim? Whatever you think is the explanation? Then . . . then justice will be done. Justice . . . yes . . . on *The Tottin Hill* Ferry."

The crowd was divided in its sympathies . . . some, those who had voted for Mr. Terwilliger, were with him. Those who had not were with Kim Chu. However, all were eager to hear the explanations.

9

The Explanations

"KIM!" THE CAPTAIN SAID. "EXPLAIN, PLEASE, HOW YOU AND YOUR friend—"

"Mae Lee," said Mae Lee. "Name—Mae Lee."

". . . how you and your friend, Mae Lee, decided that this gentleman—his honor, Mr. Terwilliger—stole your father's umbrella. For I am sure, and I suppose that all these people here congregated who have witnessed the secret in the bamboo handle are also sure, that this *is* your father's umbrella. But how did you know, how were *you* so sure that the umbrella in Mr. Terwilliger's possession was your father's? Will you explain this? Then Mr. Terwilliger must give *his* explanation."

First Kim screwed the handle back onto her father's umbrella. Then she held onto it upright in her left hand and Mae Lee, who was standing as close as possible to the heroine, touched it with her right hand. For they still were, as they had been all along, together in this, come what, come may.

Then Kim explained. As she spoke she tried not to look at the gently smiling millionaire man for she did not like to have to say the things she had to say. But, come what, come may . . . So she said, "That man must have come upstairs to the Children's Room of the library this afternoon. It was raining hard. He needed an umbrella. They didn't have one downstairs in the rack in the grown-up part so . . . he . . . crept upstairs and he saw my father's umbrella in the back left-hand square of the rack and . . . he took it . . . just plain musta took it. Because here it is!" Then Kim felt frightened. "He might have just plain borrowed it . . . thought he'd bring it back tomorrow . . . maybe . . . like the library teacher said."

"Yes," chimed in Mae Lee. "That's what he did, maybe. Just plain borrowed it. There's a sign there on the rack now. Says to just bring the umbrella back . . . no questions asked."

"Well, or else," said Kim for she felt very brave now. "Maybe the nice man knew the secret of the handle, the only one like it in the whole world, maybe."

She grew angry all over again . . . All those slaps that Grandmother had given her and the umbrella lost, perhaps forevermore! Kim's black eyes flashed.

Severely, the captain said, "Mr. Terwilliger! Did you know the secret of the handle of this umbrella?"

"No, no, no, no, no!" said Mr. Terwilliger.

"Were you in the Chatham Square Library this afternoon?" asked the captain.

"Yes, I was," said Mr. Terwilliger.

Some gasps could be heard in the gathering.

"Ah-h?" said the captain.

"Yes," said Mr. Terwilliger. "I was looking up some facts and figures for the board meeting tonight."

"Well," said the captain, taking off his hat and scratching his head. "Since when has an umbrella been called a fact and a figure?"

There was a slight sound of giggling in the gathering though most of this was caused by the laughing lady who was chuckling hard again.

"I will explain what really happened," said the millionaire man.

First he walked to the rope and took up a position there, facing the crowd. It looked as if he was about to give a speech and it was too bad that he did not have a box to stand on. Still, he was a tall man, and most could see him and certainly all could hear, for he spoke in the manner of a man accustomed to delivering speeches.

The millionaire man put his hand over his heart so all would know that what he said was the truth, the whole truth and nothing but the truth. Even though he had not been asked to swear this, he did it anyway.

"I hear he gives speeches, long ones, at the drop of a hat," said that lady in front who had made comments all along.

"Don't drop your hat, then," said some witty person next to her.

"Just the highlights, Mr. Terwilliger," the captain said and nervously examined his huge watch.

"We may be able to settle all of this out of court," said the lawyer man who had been number five of the umbrella people.

Kim was quite bewildered. All she wanted was for everybody

71

to go away and let her go home with her father's umbrella and never mind the explanations. However, she too listened curiously to the tale that the millionaire man then told . . . *his* explanation of how it was that he had Mr. Lin Chu's umbrella.

The millionaire man said, "Well, after leaving the library with the facts and figures I needed . . . see?" He produced some slips of paper and waved them at everybody to right and to left.

"He looks like a magician." Mae Lee mouthed these words to Kim.

The millionaire man went on. "Well, this young scamp, this chap . . . as I was tearing through the pouring rain because I didn't have an umbrella and I wanted to get up onto the elevated platform before I got entirely drenched . . . this young scamp rushes up to me at the bottom step and he says to me, after practically knocking me over, he says, 'Hey, mister! You're getting awfully wet. You can buy this umbrella for one dollar, just one dollar! My father sells umbrellas on Canal Street, so I go out and sell them to people like you who are caught in the rain without one.' "

Oh . . . thought Kim. That "young scamp" might have been the face-maker in the library . . . *He* must have been the one who took the umbrella and then sold it to this nice millionaire man!

The nice millionaire man continued with his speech. "So . . . I bought the young scamp's umbrella, never dawned on me it was a stolen one . . . or . . . a rare one like this of Mr. Lin Chu's. I was drenched. And I was in a terrible hurry because I heard the El coming. I tore up the stairs . . . but . . . the doors slammed in my face! You saw me," he said, pointing to Mae Lee.

"Yes," said Mae Lee. "I saw you with that big, black umbrella! And I had just come from the library and heard about the robbery and saw the sign put up. So . . ."

"So, Mr. Terwilliger . . ." the captain put in. "You never were in the Children's Room of the Chatham Square Library at all?"

"No, no, no, no, no . . ." said the millionaire man. "Just downstairs getting facts and figures."

The captain found his explanation honest and said so. "But why," he asked Kim Chu and Mae Lee curiously, "did you think that this fine gentleman had your father's umbrella . . . as indeed he did? What made you so positive . . . it looks like all these others . . ."

Mae spoke first. "We-ell . . ." she said. "First of all, the way he got on at Chatham Square . . . I decided that when he saw me on the train, he missed it on purpose . . ."

"And," said Kim, "the way he kept clutching the umbrella so tightly between his knees . . . as though he knew what a precious umbrella he had gotten hold of . . ."

"Believe me," the millionaire man said . . . still in his speech-making voice. "From now on I have to hang onto my umbrella that way. Do you know how many umbrellas I have lost in these last few rainy weeks? Seven!" he answered himself. "I leave them on ferryboats, on subways, Els and buses, in racks at the club, restaurants . . . wherever I go . . ." He smiled benignly at Kim. "There could be a town of lost umbrellas, made up mostly of mine . . ."

Kim gasped. "That's where I thought I was headed for," she said. "To the town of the lost umbrellas. I thought that's where the nickels . . ."

73

But the man didn't hear her. He was enjoying his speech. "Yes," he said, "town of the lost umbrellas. So, well . . . of course, as usual, I lost my umbrella this morning . . . oh, I don't know where . . . and I felt I must get another one by hook or by crook . . . Naturally, I leaped at the chance to buy the young scamp's. Now Bessie, my wife, will have only my trousers to press and not my coat, and I won't be scolded for losing another umbrella this morning. Because now I *have* an umbrella . . . that's what I thought. Alas! I will get scolded after all, besides having to have my pants pressed!"

"I told you he gives long speeches," said a lady. "He's after the ladies' votes now . . . I can tell . . . all that about Bessie!"

"I'm going to vote for him after all," said that lady in front.

"We-ell, I don't know," said the other. "I didn't like that 'by hook or by crook.' "

The millionaire man was winding up his discourse now. He said to Kim, "I'm glad that it was I who, unknowingly to be sure, was the one that acquired your father's umbrella, and not some one Mae Lee might not have spotted. It might have been sold to someone who would have had it blow inside out on him and would have thrown it away, cast it into a gutter!"

"Oo-ooh," breathed Kim.

"For then," continued the nice man, "then the lovely secret in the bamboo handle might have been lost forever . . . no one would have suspected it was there, any more than I did."

Kim Chu gave a wide smile. "Yes," she said. "But now you do not have an umbrella and Bessie will slap you. My father will pay you

74

back the dollar and you can buy another one. Tell Mrs. Bessie that Mr. Lin Chu will buy another umbrella."

"Oh no, no, no, no, no," said the nice millionaire man. "This story is worth a million dollars to me, and Bessie will like it, too. 'Oh, my!' she'll say."

"I will pay three nickels," repeated Kim firmly. "My father will pay the rest." She took the three buffalo nickels out of her pocket. "They have buffaloes on them," she said.

"Buffalo nickels!" exclaimed the millionaire man. "What a day! You know people in the office save buffalo nickels for me because they know my little boy, Danny, saves them? They gave me three of them this morning!"

He felt in his pocket. "Shucks!" he said. "When I was tearing for the El and reaching in my pocket for the fare, they must have popped out. I thought I heard something drop . . ."

"These must be your nickels then," said Kim in amazement. "I found them on the stairs of the El. At Chatham Square. That's where I live. I live in Chinatown. I thought the nickels said, 'Follow us! And you may find your father's umbrella.' So I did. And I did find the umbrella. And now—you find your nickels."

Kim handed the millionaire man the three nickels. "Danny will be happy," she said. "And so will my grandmother and my father."

"Fair and square," the nice man said and he pushed the nickels deep down in his pocket. He turned to leave. All the people had waited for him to disembark first, even though the rope man had lowered the rope so they could get off.

The millionaire man turned back. "Kim! How are you going to get back to Chinatown?" he asked. "Have you other nickels?" He placed a hand on Kim's shoulders. It was too bad no one had a camera.

Kim shook her head.

The captain said, "She can stay on my boat. And this will get her on the El." He handed Kim a little card. It was a pass to get on the train. Kim was glad to have it. She didn't want to crawl under the turnstile again . . . and get stuck maybe.

So the millionaire man with a wave of his arm and a bow to the captain left. Soon all the people had gone except for Kim, Mae, and the chuckling lady. The buses had waited for the passengers because the drivers were curious about the delay on the boat. They wanted to hear the umbrella story . . . every word . . . and never mind late dinners. On the Tottenville bus the cross umbrella man, number one, was sitting winding and unwinding his watch. But now he was even crosser because he had not stayed on the ferry to see the scroll and hear about the nickels.

Mae Lee didn't have to take a bus. She left last of all. "See you on Monday," she said to Kim and stepped off the boat. She paused a moment to look back at Kim. She hitched her right shoulder in the direction of the millionaire man who was hurrying up the hill, raised her right eyebrow, side-spoke the words . . . but loudly. "A great thing to act out for our next play in Chinese School!"

And she sauntered away across the wharf, nonchalantly.

The captain went back up to the helm and soon, *TOO-OOT TOO-OOT!* sounded the whistle.

Some people got on, not many at this time of the evening. Going back, the laughing lady and Kim sat in the front of the ferry. "I love the ocean," said the lady. "I spend a lot of time riding back and forth on the ferry." And she chuckled.

77

Kim chuckled, too. No wonder the lady chuckled. Who wouldn't chuckle a lot if they could ride back and forth, back and forth on the beautiful boat . . . smell the sea . . . see the gulls . . . see the lights coming on . . . the sun rising . . . the sun setting . . .

The boat lurched and lunged its way out of the slip and they were headed for home.

10

Home

KIM BREATHED A DEEP SIGH. SHE THOUGHT ABOUT HER HOMECOMING. How happy Grandmother would be to see her father's big, black umbrella back again in the corner where it always stood! Kim held the umbrella between her knees just as tightly as the millionaire man had. She looked at the city, all ablaze with lights, coming closer and closer, and at the bridges adorned with their twinkling garlands of light, and at the Statue of Liberty outlined against the late afterglow of the sunset in the west.

The laughing lady was quiet, too, and did not open her book to page forty-nine. It was too dark. Or perhaps she was napping. But suddenly she chuckled again. They were nearing the slip at the Battery. "That Terwilliger!" she said. "That Go-getter Terwilliger! Will you ever forget the way he leaped onto this boat, waving that big umbrella of yours on high?"

Kim Chu smiled. She said, "I hope he will forgive me for thinking he was a crook!"

The lady sank back into her funny thoughts and said nothing more the rest of the way. The ride back seemed to go much more slowly than the ride over. This must be because Kim was in such a hurry to put the umbrella back where it belonged and to have Grandmother smile.

Now! Here they were at last, lurching and bumping into the ferry slip at the Battery. Kim stood up, to be the first one off. She was going to be a rusher. The lady didn't stand up. She said she was going to have another round trip, see the moon, see Jupiter.

"Maybe I'll see you again some day," she said to Kim.

"Maybe," said Kim. "And my family . . ." And she got off the boat.

She turned to wave to the lady. And she waved to the captain in case he was looking. He *was* looking and he waved his hat at Kim. Then Kim rushed away to catch the El that was waiting there.

She stood close to the door all the way home, hugging the umbrella upright in front of her. Her eyes were glued to the window of the door so she would not miss the Chatham Square Station in the dark.

Dark nighttime now. Nighttime everywhere. There were some lights in some of the windows and very few had their shades pulled down. But the train went so fast Kim took in only a few of the sights. Just that the man was still looking out of his window at the scene below and his happy dog was watching the train go by. Kim knew it would not be far now, and that soon she would be home.

The train ricketty-rocketty-ed up the tracks . . . swaying . . .

Could it fly off the tracks? Go up into the air? A sky train? There! They were coming into a big station now. It was . . . she knew it was . . . the Chatham Square Station with platforms above, way up where she was, and platforms below. It seemed as though the train was not going to stop. Oh, it seemed to be going just as fast as ever. "Train! Stop!" she urged. Then suddenly, it did stop. People had to grab a strap, not to fall. The door opened and Kim plummeted out.

Clutching the umbrella she rushed down the stairs as fast as she could without tripping. She hoped she would get home before her mother and father. It seemed to her she had been gone for a week! But her parents had to stop first at Aunt Min's to pick up little Shoo-Shoo, so . . . she might get home first.

She tore through the open door of her house, up the stairs, and through her own open door. The straight chair where Grandmother always sat was closer to the door than it usually was. But Grandmother was not sitting in it!

Kim gasped. "Oo-oh-oh! Grandmother!" She tore into the other room. But Grandmother was not there either. Where was she, oh, where was she? Grandmother never went out. She was as lost as the lost umbrella had been! She must go out and look for Grandmother. Kim was about to rush back down to the outer door but then . . . Grandmother came down the hall from the rooms in front where the Wu family lived whose windows looked out on the El. Grandmother must have seen Kim from the window there.

Shuffling silently in her worn bedroom slippers she went over to her straight chair and sat down. The wrinkles in her forehead seemed deeper than ever, the blue veins in her frail hands higher. A tear wandered slowly down Grandmother's wrinkled cheek like a last raindrop winding down a window pane. Grandmother had been worried, thought Kim. For Grandmother had never, as long as Kim could remember, visited the Wus before.

Kim placed her father's umbrella straight across her grandmother's lap. With trembling fingers Grandmother gave the handle a twist, opened it, and peered in. Then she tightened it again. In Chinese she said, "I knew that you would find it."

Kim stood the umbrella in the corner where it always stood. Grandmother smiled. Kim stood beside her a moment and Grandmother put her trembling hand on Kim's forehead and said again, "I knew that you would find it."

Kim went to the open door and listened. Why didn't her family come now, this minute, so she could tell her story of the lost umbrella and how she had found it? Ah! Here they came! What a commotion on the stairs! Happy voices! Her family!

Her father was carrying many packages, her mother was carrying little Shoo-Shoo, who was chattering about something. They saw Kim standing there. And before they were even all the way up the stairs, they yelled, "Hello! Hello! Hello! See what we've brought!"

First they greeted Grandmother. Then they kissed and hugged

Kim as they always did every evening, and Shoo-Shoo flung her arms around Kim's skirts and for a time would not let her loose.

Then Grandmother stood up and shuffled over to the door, closed it, and locked it because everybody was home. Then she shuffled into the back room and brought out a low, lightweight bamboo table on which they would have dinner. Kim brought some stools from the other room and placed them around the table for people to sit on, except for Grandmother, who would have her dinner in her straight chair.

Kim's mother opened the boxes of food they had brought. "There was a wedding reception at the restaurant today," she said. "And they told us we could bring some of the good things home. And it should be good because we cooked it!"

Everybody laughed merrily.

So far, no one knew how Kim had spent the day, searching for the lost umbrella. She tried to tell the story. But everybody was too hungry to listen.

There were fortune cookies for dessert. Feeling rested and filled with good food, each one now took a cookie. Kim asked to be the last to bite into her cookie and to read her fortune. She laughed. "This is what it says," she said. " 'You will have a happy day that begins bad but ends happy!' "

"It was true! It was true!" exclaimed Kim. "And that *is* what happened!"

Now, at last, she had a chance to tell her story. She told the whole tale of the lost umbrella and she told it in Chinese so everybody, including Grandmother, would understand. You could hear a pin drop and even Shoo-Shoo did not make her little bird-like sounds.

They made Kim tell the story again and again and she did, filling in the gaps with each telling. Then she stood up and she acted out the story, now in English. She was herself in this play, she was Mae Lee, the millionaire man, then the laughing lady—everybody chuckled a lot hearing about her—the captain, the man with the rope . . . she was all of them.

Then she showed her family the pass to ride on the El that the captain had given her. "I shall put it in a secret place," she said, "so I will not lose it."

"Yes," said her father. "But not in the bamboo handle of my umbrella." He picked Kim up in his arms and hugged her tightly, and then her mother hugged her tightly, tightly.

Now Kim's mother and father and Grandmother began to speak to one another in the same sort of sign language that Kim and Mae spoke in . . . the lift of an eyebrow, the curve of a lip, and the hitch of a shoulder. Grandmother stood up then, opened the palms of her hands as though to catch raindrops, and shuffled off to bed.

That night, in the cot that she shared with Shoo-Shoo, Kim thought about the whole day. It seemed like a dream and she couldn't go to sleep, remembering it all, reliving it step by step, telling herself the story, again and again, feeling for the pass on the El that she had tucked beneath the mattress.

She put her arms around her little sister. "You know, Shoo-Shoo," she murmured, "I was on a ferryboat today."

Shoo-Shoo answered sleepily. "I was on a fairy boat, too, to-morrow."

"Will go . . . some day . . ." Kim corrected her.

"Will . . . some day . . ." repeated Shoo-Shoo softly.

And they both fell sound asleep.